ANYA BELTSINA

IN A BIG AND NOISY CITY

Traffic Light Story

In a big and noisy city
all the houses looked pretty.
Cars ran round really fast.
People walked from dawn to dusk

In the middle of it all
on a large and metal pole
stood a traffic light, so bright.
It worked hard all day and night.
All the signals: green, red, and yellow
were hardworking and keen fellows.

STOP!

Green light had a happy soul.
He cried: "Go! Move! Drive! Stroll!"
Everybody loved green light.
He shone bright with all his might.

Yellow light was quite mellow,
but a worried, watchful fellow.
He made everyone prepare,
and hold back with cautious care.

Red light made
 the whole street stop.
He was tougher
 than a cop!

One odd morning in the city
where the houses looked pretty,
all the cars drove really fast,
and pedestrians would pass,
red light said, "It has to stop!"
He was stubborn as a snob!
Red got tired of his job
to make cars and people stop.

Yellow light was quite mellow.
He seemed softer than a marshmallow.
It turned out that bright yellow
was a jealous, bitter fellow!

Yellow said: "I cannot stand
life without a command!
BE PREPARED! CAREFUL!
are not orders, just some rules.
All I wish that I could be
taken much more seriously!
I do not enjoy my role!
I just want some more control!"
No one knew that yellow light
felt so selfish, full of spite.

11

Green light was the happy one.
He was always having fun.
That green merry, joyful guy
had the need to clarify
to both red and yellow lights:
"It is time to stop the fights!"
Green light told the other two
something simple but so true.

He reminded red bright light:
"Do not fight! Just watch the site!
Safety first! No need to sob!
Angry fighting has to stop!
Every signal has a function
to keep safe this busy junction!

13

14

"Traffic lights: red, yellow, and green,
we are a powerful machine.
Signal green, you know me,
I let everyone feel free.

"Yellow light
could be more mellow
but an important
and cautious fellow.

"People know when they see
red light shining bright with glee
to stop moving, cease and freeze.
Red means STOP! DON'T GO! PLEASE!

"Kids, be careful in the city
where the houses look pretty,
and the cars drive all day long!
Follow rules and move along!"

FRUIT AND VEGGIE FEUD

In a big and noisy store
    in the middle of main floor
fruit and veggies lived together
    during rain and sunny weather.

They were brought from many countries,
some from tropics with tall palm trees.
Avocadoes, plums, and grapes
all of them had different shapes.
All bright colors of the fruit
were just brilliant, so cute.

One odd morning they all woke
and decided as a joke
to find out which of them
was most popular and glam.

First to speak was not an apple,
but a proudful pineapple:
"I am fabulous and grand!
I come from a charming plant.
I have seen exotic lands
with best beaches and white sands."

Kiwi, mango, and dragon fruit
got involved in that dispute:
"We all lived in far, far lands."
"We all saw palm trees and sand!"
"Fruits of tropics are delicious!"
"We are tasty, sweet, and nutritious!"

Veggies waited long enough.
They were trying to be tough.
Carrots jumped in first of all.
They were always on a roll:
"We are fabulous and cool!"
"Kids love bringing us to school!"
"We help people's eyes and hearts."
"We are chiefs of shopping carts!"

Peppers, broccoli and chards
suddenly were caught off guard:
"We are colorful and tasty!"
"There is no need to be hasty!"
"Veggies are important foods
more substantial than fruit!"

"Wait a minute, everyone!
We agreed to have some fun!"
said one bright and red tomato
winking to his friend potato.
He explained that all of them
were so fabulous and glam!

"Cabbage, celery, and spinach
make kids strong like stellar gymnasts!
Okra, kale, and snow peas
have more calcium than cheese."

Their red tomato friend
    wanted for that feud to end.
He told each and everyone
    to stop yelling and have fun!

"All the veggies and the fruit
whether tropical or root
have unique and tasty flavors
any kid or parent savors.
What's the best of all the food?
Something healthy, tasty, and good.
All kids know that they should
eat their veggies and their fruit!"

Beltsina Anya.
In a big and noisy city. – 2021. – 34 p.

....

Book for children

6+

By Anya Beltsina
In a big and noisy city

Illustrations by Kristina Yolkina

Ordering Information:
For details, contact theanyabeltsina@gmail.com.

Print ISBN: 978-1-66782-697-4

Printed in the United States of America.

Second Edition